For: Pat
May you always hear the call
of the still small voice of
Jesus!

Blessings!
December 1, 2002

Judi Brantley

Steven Brantley

Given to:

By:

On:

For the Father of glory.
For the Brantley lineage.
J.S.B & T.S.B.

To the glory of God and our Savior Jesus Christ who abolished death.
In memory of my mother, Jean McDaniel.
C.M.C.

*". . . I am the resurrection and the life: he that believeth in me, though he were dead,
yet shall he live . . . " John 11:25*

The Legend of
Snowflake
The Messenger Deer

Written by
Judi and Steven Brantley

Paintings by
Carol McDaniel-Clark

Spring House Books   Wadmalaw Island, South Carolina

Christmas again soon was coming, decorations filled the stores and the street.
Hustle and bustle and worry, read the faces of the shoppers He'd meet.

Might this be the year they would hear, His story so long and so sweet?
The story of Christmas and Easter, done once, without need to repeat.

Could He convince them to help Him? Would they stop and give Him some time?
The old, old story was worth telling; angels deemed His story—sublime!

The world's tension was mounting and weighty, growing heavier with each passing day.
Bearing the burden of sadness and worry, He withdrew to a quiet place to pray.

"Father, show Me how I might reach them, how to tell the story anew:
The story they've heard through the ages, of Your great wondrous love, so true."

"My Son—first You try it the old way, touching their hearts and their minds to succeed.
If after You've tried, they're found wanting, We'll try something more radical indeed!"

His Father was really the reason that Christmas had begun,
From the Father's heart—to His children, the Father sent His Son.

Through the years, the world had forgotten, due to hustle, bustle, and worry.
It was time to remind them, *"Christmas Is Peace!"* not shopping, stress, and scurry.

"... when he bringeth in the firstbegotten into the world, he saith, And let all the angels of God worship him." Hebrews 1:6

Using a still, small voice like the Father, Jesus began, with great hope, His quest,
For someone to tell the Christmas tree story, for someone to tell it the best:

Will you tell My story, the story of the tree? Will you tell My story, will you tell it for Me!
If you tell My story, the story of the tree, children can see Christmas and also Calvary.

Jesus softly asked the baker, who was busily baking his bread,
Will you stop mixing and kneading, and tell My story for Me instead?

The baker would not answer, going right on with his work,
After patiently waiting, He moved on and asked a clerk.

"And Jesus said unto them, I am the bread of life..." John 6:35

Will you tell My story, the story of the tree? Will you tell My story, will you tell it for Me?
By telling My story, the story of the tree, many may come to know how they, too, can be free.

The clerk was counting her money. Approaching, Jesus could sense her fear.
He spoke words intended to comfort, and He knew she had ears to hear.

The clerk was wrapped up by the things of the world—tight in the arms of the Charmer,
Like lightning, God's angels came forth to do war; and on went His quest, to a farmer.

Coming into the land of the farmer, Jesus admired the sunflowers that grew
And thought, *Perhaps the farmer will be My answer, for telling My story anew.*

Will you tell My story, the story of the tree? Will you tell My story, will you tell it for me?
When you tell My story, the story of the tree, children young and old may see how growing
with God can be.

In the quiet of the day of plentiful yield, when the sun was almost down,
Jesus sat with him in the garden, seeking help—but receiving a frown.

Saddened by the farmer's choice, Jesus watched as the world grew worse.
After praying with His Father, He went forth to find a nurse.

He saw her caring for patients—always using the Father's touch.
He saw her teaching the lame to walk, while leaving behind—their crutch.

He walked with her every minute, He whispered His love for her every day,
My child, if you'll do My bidding, I have a new plan for sharing My way.

"Oh, Lord! I know how You love us, but—I'm not good with words, I fear.
Please find someone else for Your story." Jesus turned and shed a tear.

Forever and for always—unable to hold a grudge,
Persistently pursuing, Jesus sought for His cause a judge.

Jesus entered the judge's chambers, going in through the wide, open door.
He quietly watched the judge ponder those who came here—rich and poor.

Jesus knew the judge loved the Father and often prayed on bended knee,
Hopeful, He asked him to tell the world the story of the Christmas tree.

Will you tell My story, the story of the tree? Will you tell My story, will you tell it for Me?
If you tell My story, the story of the tree, many will meet their Pardon and also their Plea.

The judge would not mix church and state: "No! I cannot be a preacher."
Courage propelled Jesus on, searching now instead, for a teacher.

"I am the door: by me if any man shall enter in, he shall be saved. . ." John 10:9

He found a teacher at school grading papers, feeling proud of what she taught,
Telling children to always seek knowledge, then teaching children what they sought.

He explained His situation. She replied, "Lord, you know the rule.
I must be careful what I teach—no praying or preaching at school!"

Profane was the rule that she spoke. Of all the stories she taught—His should be one,
For His story could change a life and help more than anything—under the sun.

When the ones who know have grown fearful, how could others come to know it?
Smiling, He thought of one who might help, a songwriter and a poet.

Jesus stood as the poet wrote a poem, carefully creating sentences that rhyme,
Knowing from where the talent came, Jesus wondered, *Would the poet give the
Source some time?*

Presenting His proposal to the poet, pleading with him for to tell,
His answer: "It is quite good, Your story, Lord, but—I don't think it will sell!"

For years He had asked His children for help—every nation had turned Him down,
He walked and He wept and remembered, the Cross and the thorns of His crown.

In his heart, Jesus knew they had heard His call, yet on with their own work they went.
Some would not even acknowledge Him, and the others did not want to be sent.

Christmas again soon was coming, the time was ripe for the people to see,
Eternal life is the promise of Christmas, symbolized by the evergreen tree.

Now who would tell His story, and why from heaven He did come down?
Rememb'ring what His Father had said, He walked toward the woods, from town.

As Jesus walked deep in the woodland, He found what He knew He would find,
Animals encircled by angels, each loving Him with its whole heart and mind.

He then shared His heart with this kingdom, His Father's creation so grand:
"Our plan requires a miracle—and a touch of the Father's hand."

The animals knelt down before Him; though He was quiet, His heart did cry out,
Where are the people who love Me? People who know what My story's about?

"Man has ceased listening to man, man has ceased listening to Me.
Yet we cannot cease trying to tell them, My story—the story of the tree.

"None of you in the animal kingdom, not a deer or a dove had a doubt;
Rabbits never trusted the things of the world, loved money, or prestige, or clout.

"You've all always known who I am, why I came down and what I have done,
And for a purpose, you have been called, like the angels, stars, and the sun.

"One of you shall soon share My story, with a child, in search of a tree,
I will gladly commission your choice from among you; now, whom will it be?

"As you may know, in the days of old, parents taught their children by decree.
We'll reverse the order of teaching, when a child tells the story of the tree.

"All the children who gathered around Me, in the olden days—in Galilee,
They all grew up great listeners and learners, gaining their knowledge on bended knee.

"By your teaching and telling the children, why from heaven I was sent,
One day they may reach their parents, who will turn from their natural bent."

As the angels guided and prodded, the animals soon made their choice;
Jesus quietly watched and waited for whom would receive human voice.

A most beautiful white deer, named Snowflake, won the sacred vote.
She knelt at His feet, and He touched her, gently rubbing her coat.

With His strong, gentle hand upon her, He began His blessing and prayer:
"Father, I thank You for Your creation, and their willingness to go forth and share.
I ask for Your greatest blessing as Snowflake goes out in Your care.
I trust You to place in her path, the child who's yearning—and dost dare,
To ask the mysterious question, why at Christmas, a tree, they prepare?
For Your blessings, I thank You, Father, and for the hearts You have given Me to spare.

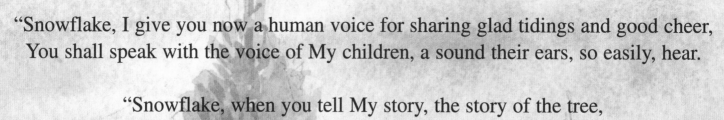

"Snowflake, I give you now a human voice for sharing glad tidings and good cheer,
You shall speak with the voice of My children, a sound their ears, so easily, hear.

"Snowflake, when you tell My story, the story of the tree,
The promise starts before Eden, fulfilled on Calvary.

"The tree of life from Eden, and the tree taken from the wood,
Stand for the Cross of Calvary, where for them, alone, I stood.

"And like the stories of Christmas and Easter, intertwined, ne'er to be unwound,
My love I will wrap around them, forever seeking 'til, at last, I am found.

"Christmas celebrates My birthday, and Abba's love for sending His Son.
Easter celebrates freedom from death, that for them, on the Cross, I won.

"And whosoever liveth and believeth in me shall never die. Believest thou this?" John 11:26

"A beautiful stage will be set for you, a special child will listen with her heart,
God will perform a great miracle, as you are put in place to play your part.

"Many details for the night will be missing, just trust Us with those, We do ask,
Remember—nothing is impossible for God; for Him, this is quite a small task."

His soft, warming light filled the woodland, His glory shone all around,
After one more prayer and a blessing, He was once more heaven bound.

Children have a special connection, to animals and angels, you see,
Heaven thought it only proper and fitting, they all share the story of the tree.

"... and a little child shall lead them." Isaiah 11:6

Published by
Spring House Books
Wadmalaw Island, South Carolina

Edited by: Pringle Franklin Mt. Pleasant, South Carolina

Author Acknowledgments
We give special thanks to Pringle Franklin for her editorial advice and Biblical insights. She is a Godsend.
And to Jon Verdi for his expertise and guidance in layout. He is a blessing.
And to all those who have faithfully covered this project in prayer.

Artist Acknowledgments
With many thanks to my models: Adair, Bill, Cameron, Clara, David, Deanne, Douglas, Edwina, Elizabeth, Ellen, Freddie, Graham, Hannah, Joanna, Maddy, Meagan, Michael, Sarah C., Sarah J., Sarah R., T.C., Tiffany, and Tonya.

First Printing 2002

Scripture quoted is from THE HOLY BIBLE, The Authorized King James Version.

Typesetting and Formatting by: Jon Verdi Graphic Design.

Printed in Hong Kong by C & C Offset Printing Company, Ltd.

Library of Congress Catalog Card Number: 00-90589

ISBN 1-892570-04-1

10 9 8 7 6 5 4 3 2 1